GOOD FRIENDS

GOOD FRIENDS

An Avery Barks Dog Mystery

Mary Hiker

Good Friends Copyright © 2015
By Mary Hiker

Printed in the United States of America
First Printing, 2015

Good Friends - Mary Hiker – 1st ed.

ISBN-13: 978-1518614095
ISBN-10: 1518614094

Published By Awesome Dog

www.MaryHiker.com

Dedicated to the Creator of all the animals.

Chapter 1

It's gonna be a boomer.

My blistered hands gripped the rake a little tighter as I scooped up the last of the twigs and small branches, piling them in the back of the utility trailer. The temperature dropped as dark puffy clouds approached with a far off rumble and the wind speed picked up, sure signs an afternoon thunder storm was about to burst out of the early summer sky. My dog, Chevy, and I were about to be right in the middle of it.

My navy t-shirt was still a bit damp from a rain shower earlier in the day. I'd worked right though that one and enjoyed the water as it cooled my body in the most natural way. But lightning was a whole different story. I'd heard about more than one person getting zapped by a bolt in these mountains and I didn't plan to be one of them.

I called my dog so we could get back to the campground's main lodge before the storm hit. The Golden Retriever mix bounded out from one of the campsites I'd been cleaning and jumped in the utility trailer's passenger seat as I started the engine. Oversized raindrops bounced off the front of the gator as I hit the gas and headed across ninety-eight acres toward the Friendly Bear Campground Lodge. Chevy barked and tried to catch the rain in his mouth as we sped toward shelter.

The sky opened and rain pelted my face and body, completely soaking my t-shirt and jeans in a matter of seconds. I barely managed to keep the water out of my eyes while I drove and water flowed off both my ponytail and Chevy's fur by the time we made it to the main building.

I jumped off the gator and onto the covered porch of the main lodge, creating a puddle of rainwater on the wooden planks underneath my feet. Chevy followed behind and shook his body furiously, releasing the rain from his golden fur and splattering water across the rocking chairs that sat in front of us. The fresh smell of rain was overtaken by a smell only animal lovers could love – wet dog.

It was my fifth day in a row working at the campground and adjoining acreage to help my old friend, Tonya, get ready for camping season. She let me camp anytime I wanted - for free. It was a perk that came in handy when my cousin brought her five kids out to the mountains every year – so it was the least I could do. Besides, it was nice to hang out at the empty campground before season started and let Chevy have free run to explore the place.

Most years, I would help out for a day or two preparing campsites for visitors, but this year was different. A big kickoff event was scheduled for this weekend and the entire property had been rented out. Both the campground area and a new area for outdoor events needed to be in prime condition for the party. The festival would be a big financial boost to the campground and get the season started off right for Tanya.

The flap on the lodge's doggie door opened and a black and white Border Collie bounded out to greet Chevy. The two dogs chased each other across the porch until Chevy's hind end knocked over a flowerpot, spilling fresh dirt across the wooden planks.

"Hey, Gunner," I said and bent down to scoop up Chevy's mess.

The friendly Border Collie pawed at my arm as I scraped the dirt back into the clay pot. His eyes penetrated mine as I softly gripped his paw and gave him a little handshake, water dripping from my clothes and hair. Gunner gave me a quick lick on the cheek before Chevy flew by holding a tug toy and sideswiped the both of us. Gunner turned and grabbed the end of the red rubber toy hanging out of Chevy's mouth and the two dogs started a game of tug-o-war.

The lodge door opened and a tanned arm reached out, tossing me some old towels.

"Thanks Tonya," I said and wiped the water from my face with the softest one. "I'll try and get Chevy dried off before I come in."

Tonya stepped out onto the porch, laughing. "Don't worry about it, those two will be playing for a good hour – they always do." Her shoulder length blond hair was frizzy with the humidity and she had the trim build of a natural athlete. "My floors need to be mopped, anyway. Just get the big drops off him and I'll clean up when they calm down a bit."

I smiled. Tonya was a big animal lover and a wet dog wouldn't put a damper on her day. She'd been a friend of mine for quite a while. We met back in college and I'd always been impressed by her intelligence and positive attitude. She had a laid-back personality but ran the campground with a business mind.

Her dog was as smart as most humans I knew. I'd tried several times to get Tonya to train Gunner for search and rescue missions, but she'd always refused. Mainly, because she didn't like the idea of working alone in the woods during the middle of the night – something that was the norm in my search and rescue work.

I ran the towel across Chevy's soaked fur, then squeezed the excess water out of my navy t-shirt and followed my friend inside the lodge as the dogs raced past me and rain pelted the green metal roof. "Whew, it's really coming down out there."

I hung the dripping towels on one of the hooks in the mudroom, adding to the wet outerwear that graced the wall and kicked off my squishy sneakers.

As I entered the main foyer of the lodge, I was startled by a slight smell that was definitely out of place out here at the campground. I stood for a minute and focused on the scent.

Yep, it was definitely men's cologne - the expensive kind that only the city guys wore. I'd only smelled this version once before, about two years prior. It was the day I traveled to Asheville to buy my truck and was forced to sit next to the dealership's sales manager for close to two hours while we worked out a deal. He reeked of the stuff.

It had to be Jacob Tanner.

Chapter 2

An extremely fit man in his late forties walked out of Tonya's office and into the lodge's main entry area. Jacob Tanner wore the casual business attire that car dealers in this region generally wore. A blue button up-shirt fresh from the dry cleaners with a perfect crease down each arm, pressed khakis and shiny dark brown loafers. No tie, because we were in the North Carolina mountains, after-all.

Jacob sported a tan that undoubtedly came from spending many afternoons golfing at the high-end resorts in the region. I was glad to smell that he had learned to ease off on the sheer amount of cologne that he'd worn the last time I saw him. He was sociable, beyond handsome and smelled expensive, but his hard-core business demeanor made me uncomfortable. Jacob just had too much type-A personality going on for my taste.

He was inspecting the campground before the big event for his long-time boss and friend, 'Big Diesel' Bronson. They had a standard that was gold level and Tonya was under a lot of pressure to produce a quality environment for their festival.

"I'll be right back with you, Jacob," Tonya said as she scooted past the office and down a wide hallway.

I followed behind her as my soaked socks left wet footprints on the old wooden floors.

Jacob nodded. "Hi, Avery. " He didn't try to hide a wide grin as he watched the water drip from my clothes.

Before I could respond, Chevy ran up to Jacob and leaned his wet furry body against the man's legs in a friendly greeting, causing his fancy pressed pants to get wet. Jacob jumped back and I held my breath until I heard his raucous laughter.

"Good thing I'm a dog lover, buddy," he said and patted Chevy's wet head. I waved him a friendly good-bye.

I followed Tonya to a back room that was decorated with just enough items to provide a comfortable cabin feel. She used the bedroom on the summer nights she stayed at the campground.

Tonya pointed to a closet. "I've got some extra t-shirts and shorts in there. Go ahead and change into some dry clothes." She handed me a wicker laundry basket for my wet clothes. "I also have a little gift for you and Chevy sitting on the second shelf. It's a thank-you for helping me out all week."

I was sorting through the clean clothes looking for something that would fit me when Tonya's phone rang.

"Hello, Friendly Bear Campground."

She listened for a minute and gasped. "Are you sure?"

The phone clunked on the floor and Tonya grabbed her jacket off the bed as she bolted from the room. A moment later, the front door slammed shut.

Concerned, I reached down for the phone, "Hello?"

"Avery?"

It was Deputy Don Donaldson's familiar voice. He was a member of my search and rescue team and a good friend.

"Don? What's going on?"

The front door opened and slammed shut again, I assumed Jacob followed Tonya outside.

"I've been out this way following up on a burglary call..." The wind blew into his phone as he spoke. "I just found a dead body leaning up against the campground's main gate."

Chapter 3

Chevy and Gunner napped on the dog beds scattered across the floor of Tonya's office as I relaxed in her cushy chair and slid my gift onto the desk. A cute teddy bear sat on the edge of Tonya's desk holding a little sign that read 'Thank You. Hope this starts a new friendship, Jacob.' I wondered if that was normal business practice for Jacob or if he had a thing for Tonya.

I leaned back and turned on the evening news with the remote, wondering if they'd announce the body found out at the entrance gate. Instead, Big Diesel's latest car commercial blared from the TV.

"Hi Y'all, it's Big Diesel Bronson and I've got some big news for you! I'm officially off the market. That's right, Miss Lilly promised her hand in marriage and we're throwin' a party..."

That's why I've been working my tail off at Tonya's campground, I thought, glancing at the blisters on my hands.

Big Diesel was a middle-aged gentle giant with puffs of grey hair peeking out from the sides of his trucker cap. His six-foot five-inch frame and two-hundred seventy pounds filled out his trademark bib overalls and he usually had a cheek full of tobacco.

His farmer look was all about marketing, since he was actually born in the City of Raleigh and owned several large car dealerships across the region. He had a huge bank account and a reputation for generosity. From the size of Miss Lilly's engagement ring flashing on the TV screen, he planned on being with her for a very long time.

Miss Lilly was a forty-something widower with a perfect complexion and even better manners. Her thick dark hair flowed perfectly to her shoulders and set off her bright blue eyes. She was one of the sweetest ladies in the county and it sounded like Big Diesel had landed himself a good woman.

The car dealer leaned in to the camera as the commercial came to a close. "Come on out to our engagement festival this weekend at Friendly Bear Campground and get a great deal on a truck while you're there. We'll have lots of great vehicles parked out in the pasture to choose from."

I chuckled. Big Diesel was a salesman through and through.

My phone rang and Deputy Don's number appeared on my caller ID.

"Hey Don, what's the latest on the body?"

"Boy, I'll tell you what... Big Diesel sure has a lot of pull," he said, sounding a bit flustered. "I've been ordered by the Sheriff to investigate this death undercover - no news of the body is to be made public until after the festival this weekend."

"Amazing what money can do these days," I said and leaned back even further in the chair. "I wondered why Jacob Tanner tore off down the driveway after Tonya."

"Yeah, he was already on his cell phone when he drove by me at the gate." I could hear the rain beating on Don's truck hood in the background. "Anyway, I just wanted to ask you not to mention this to anyone for now."

"The old boys network sure runs deep around here." I said and scratched Chevy's head when he plopped it on my lap. "Who was it that died, anyway?"

Lightning flashed outside the window.

"I don't know his identity, yet." He said and blew out a deep breath. "And they're not going to make it easy for me to find out. I'll talk to you later."

I hung up the phone just as the office door flew open.

Chapter 4

Tonya's breathing was labored from sprinting up the gravel drive. "I sure didn't need that surprise today." She stood in her cabin office, toweling off her hair.

She had a lot riding on this event and wouldn't want any news of a dead body to get out any more than Big Diesel and his boys. Tonya would get a nice chunk of the festival profits and planned to use it to build a dog friendly area for the campground.

Big Diesel already supplied the land grading equipment to prep several acres of her land for the weekend's festival and truck show. After it was over, Tonya would get the benefit of having most of the prep work done for her new dog park area. If the festival bombed, Tonya would have to reimburse him for the work. Extra money I didn't think she had.

"Everything should be all right," she said and vigorously rubbed the towel back and forth across her head.

At this rate, her entire stash of towels and dry clothes would be used up before the end of the night. Gunner woke from his nap, stretched and sauntered over to welcome her back inside.

"The Sheriff and Big Diesel grew up together," Tonya said and bent down to pet her dog. "He's got the news about the body on lock down."

I looked at her with a raised eyebrow. "Doesn't it make you nervous that there was a shooting close by?"

"Deputy Don said the guy broke into Mel Medlock's house and got shot in the process. He must've dropped dead in front of the gate." Her shoulders relaxed a bit as she exhaled. "They already know who shot him and why, they just need to find out who he is."

"Mel admitted to it?"

"Sounds like he was darn proud of it," she said over her shoulder as she headed to the back bedroom to find some dry clothes, Gunner plodding behind. "The guy robbed his brand new safe and Mel found him standing in his living room - self-defense all the way."

That news didn't surprise me all that much. Even though the man was in his late fifties, Mel Medlock was an ex-marine and one tough son of a gun. I had no doubt in his ability to protect his home and family, even if it cost him his own life.

"What if the Medlock's let the cat out of the bag?"

"They won't." Tonya sounded confident. "Not with the pile of cash they're getting from Big Diesel to keep quiet for a couple days. You know Mel, he always looks for the best deal he can get."

I shook my head and silently reminded myself never to get on Big Diesel's bad side.

"Is Heather okay?" I asked, suddenly worried about Mel's wife. "She must be scared to death."

"She wasn't home." Tonya's eyes grew big when the realization hit. "She probably hasn't heard about it yet."

Heather was a well-proportioned woman with soft features and a good twenty years younger than Mel. The poor woman still dealt with occasional panic attacks related to a previous break-in by her ex-boyfriend. I always thought Mel was a good man for her, any woman would feel safer whenever he was around.

Chevy put his front paws on my lap and demanded my attention. He strained his neck, reaching over the desk until his nose touched my gift box. I laughed and rubbed my own nose when the smell of wet dog fur wafted up from his golden body. Based on his high interest, I suspected there was some type of dog treat in the box.

The soft blue wrapping paper was decorated with Golden Retriever puppies. "Nice touch," I said to Tonya as she re-entered the office and I opened the gift.

My dog watched intently until he could contain himself no longer and buried his nose inside the box, emerging with an oatmeal dog treat. He trotted over to the corner of the office with his prize and sat down for a snack. I grabbed a dog treat from the cookie jar on Tonya's desk and tossed it to Gunner so he wouldn't feel deprived.

After pushing aside three layers of colorful tissue paper, I pulled out a small doggie cam. It was the latest gadget that hangs from the dog's collar and records video from the dog's perspective.

"Thanks Tonya, that's a perfect gift." I laughed

and held up the small camera. "It'll be entertaining watching Chevy's antics on the computer screen."

"I just wanted to thank you for all the hard work." Tonya's eyes lit up as her focus returned to the campground event. "Jacob was pretty pleased with the place during his inspection and just left me a short to-do list."

"Anything you need help with?"

"Nope," she said and wrapped a towel around her wet head. "He's decided my office is too small and is taking over my maintenance building for his fair headquarters. I just need to get him a set of keys for the new office and take some extra tables down there for the rest of his guys."

"All right, I'll see you this weekend then." Chevy jumped up beside me as I stood, his oatmeal stick hanging out of his mouth, already half eaten.

Tonya hesitated for a minute then asked, "You know, Deputy Don seems like a level headed guy... and good looking too."

I put my hands on my hips and gave her the 'oh no, you just didn't' look. "I don't think about him that way." I chuckled, then headed for the door.

Don was my friend and a co-volunteer on the search and rescue team, It wouldn't be good to even think about crossing that line.

"Well, if you're not interested in him, will you poke around and see if he might be interested in me?" Tonya's green eyes were full of hope.

She obviously didn't realize that most guys in the county had a crush on her.

"I'll give it a try," I said, surprised at the sudden irritation that made me cringe as I walked out the door.

Chapter 5

Bluegrass music filled the air as the local band played while Chevy and I strolled into the festival. The smell of burgers cooking on a grill reminded me I hadn't eaten lunch and made my stomach growl. My dog pulled on his leash, attempting to drag me to meet and greet every person that got within ten feet. If Chevy had been born human, he would've made a great politician.

Several folks without much flexibility danced in front of the stage and many more sat in folding chairs enjoying the music under the shade of expansive maple trees. Tonya and Gunner were busy leading a kids' pet parade around the edge of the property as parents watched and clapped for the children as they walked by.

Food and game booths were jammed next to each other in a long lane and kiddie rides entertained the young ones. The newly renovated east pasture held a slew of new trucks on display straight from Big Diesel's car dealership. But the center of attention for most of the male population in attendance was definitely the classic car show.

I stood taking in the scene and watched a toddler wobble by holding an ice cream cone in one hand and grabbing his mom's shorts with the other. He was in awe of Chevy and pointed to my dog's furry face with his melting treat.

"Mama! Dog!"

Chevy wrongly assumed the treat held in front of his face was meant for him and devoured the ice cream cone in one swift gulp. He licked his chops with happy satisfaction and the kid stood open-mouthed as his mother tried to keep from laughing.

Red faced, I quickly apologized for my glutton of a dog and offered to buy the kid a new cone to keep the peace. Chevy followed me over to the ice cream truck and I reached into my back pocket to pay, but came up with nothing. Funny, I could've sworn I'd stuffed about fifty bucks in there as I walked into the campground. I checked my other pockets. They were empty too.

Must've fallen out, I thought.

My face flushed as I turned to tell the mother the bad news...no cash for ice cream, when a man's muscular arm reached up to the window with a five dollar bill and paid for me.

I turned and saw my deputy friend. "Thanks Don. I think I dropped my money."

"No problem." He handed the fresh cone to the toddler as I kept a firm grip on Chevy's leash.

"How's the investigation going?"

"The deceased had a long rap sheet, including break-ins and lived over two hundred miles away in Raleigh." Don wiped ice cream drips off his hand. "We're just waiting on confirmation that the bullet matches Mr. Medlock's gun."

We strolled over to the classic car show and found the crowd of folks buzzing about a huge cash prize for the competition. Entrants rushed about putting last minute touches on their classics, shining the chrome and wiping down the spotless interiors.

A small crowd gathered around a giant wooden sign that towered over the entrance to the classic car competition area. Excited chatter from the crowd centered around two things. First: this car show was being run under a unique set of rules that fit the engagement party atmosphere. Second: there was a cash prize of ten thousand dollars.

The sign stated the simplified rules as such:

1. Miss Lilly is Judge.

2. There is One Criteria for the Prize: Best Display Showing Your Love of Cars.

That was it.

Sounds like a rule that Miss Lilly would embrace, I thought. She was all about love and joy.

Don and I walked amongst the refurbished cars and he stared intently at the sleek engines while I focused on keeping Chevy a safe distance from the vehicles. If there's one thing Chevy likes more than eating ice cream, it's riding in the car.

An intercom crackled with the announcement that Big Diesel and Miss Lilly were on their way and judging would begin in a couple minutes. Tonya hustled over after finishing the pet parade and was getting in position to help at the car competition.

As she walked past, she glanced at Don and gave me a wink. I got distracted and loosened my grip on Chevy's leash, just as Leonard Cates opened the door to his cherry red muscle car. He had a cloth in his hand ready to wipe down the dash one last time.

Chevy heard the car door open, pulled away from me, bounded into Leonard's car and stuck his head out the window. He looked out at the crowd and let out a gleeful bark. Leonard gasped and sputtered while Chevy bobbed his head and pranced in the shiny red seat.

I was mortified and hoped my dog hadn't just cost him the prize.

Leonard furiously tried to lure Chevy out of his car with no luck, spun around to me and shook his finger.

"Avery, get your darn dog out of my car!" Leonard growled as the veins near his temples bulged. "I'm trying to win ten thousand dollars here."

I moved toward the car, but was stopped in my tracks when Big Diesel and Miss Lily walked up hand-in-hand to judge the classics. I felt my face get hot as my dog planted himself firmly in Leonard's car.

Leonard shot me a death stare as Chevy stuck his head out the window with a happy face and gave a 'Let's go!' bark as he waited for a ride.

Big Diesel shook his head and tried to hide a grin. "You're gonna have a time getting all that dog fur outta your car, Leonard."

The crowd and other car entrants nodded and snickered as they gathered around Big Diesel and Miss Lilly.

Leonard glared at me. "I know."

"Ohhhhh my goodness," a sweet southern female voice broke the tension.

Miss Lilly clutched her chest and ran to the window

of Leonard's car, her big engagement ring sparkling in the sunlight. "And who are you?" she asked and cradled Chevy's face between her hands.

My dog responded with a kiss on Miss Lilly's cheek.

The southern belle sighed, turned to Big Diesel and proclaimed, "My love, I do not need to go any further. There is no one in this entire world that loves riding in a car as much as this sweet dog."

Big Diesel chuckled, put his arm around her waist, leaned over and gave her a big smooch on the lips.

Miss Lilly reached for the over-sized blue winner's ribbon from Big Diesel's hand and placed it on Leonard's entry stand. "I just love the look of joy on a dog's face when they ride in a car."

Rumblings and whispers rose into a crescendo from the crowd of classic car enthusiasts. I pushed through the crowd, opened Leonard's car door and Chevy bounded out. This time, I wrapped his leash around my wrist a couple times to avert any more disasters.

Big Diesel made a big show of it as he stepped up to a makeshift podium and pulled the ten thousand dollar check from his shirt pocket.

He adjusted his bib-overalls, tapped on the portable microphone and bellowed. "Boys, I warned you this wasn't a regular car show!"

The crowd hooted and hollered.

"My precious Lilly has chosen a winner based on the love of cars." Big Diesel took out a pen and put Leonard's name on the check. "Isn't loving cars a great thing?"

The spectators whistled and cheered.

"That was some great creativity, Leonard," Big Diesel said as the men shook hands and Miss Lilly joined in posing for pictures for the local newspaper.

After the photo-op was complete and the lovebirds started to work the crowd, Leonard came over and patted Chevy on the head. "Thanks, Buddy."

The new classic car champ gave me a big smile and a hug to let me know all was forgiven and I breathed a sigh of relief, knowing I wouldn't be getting any auto cleaning bills in the mail.

As several excited car enthusiasts converged on Leonard with congratulations, I realized I'd lost track of my friend, Don. I glanced around and found him leaning against the side of the podium talking on his cell phone.

"Yes, I'm sure Mr. Medlock used his hunting rifle." He spoke into his phone and held his hand to his head "Are you sure...?"

Don hung up, shook his head and frowned.

"What's wrong?"

"This death investigation has taken a nose dive," Don said, the frown spreading further across his forehead. "The deceased now has a name, D. Leonardo. He had Mel Medlock's gold watch in his pocket, but the sixty thousand dollars missing from Mel's safe is nowhere to be found."

"Maybe he dropped it after Mel shot him."

Don's shoulders lifted with tension and his brows furrowed even deeper.

"That's not all." Don looked out over the noisy crowd. "Mel Medlock didn't kill the intruder. The death bullet was shot at close range from a handgun – a nine millimeter."

Chapter 6

I let Chevy off leash as we approached the Campground office and he romped ahead of us to find his buddy, Gunner. Don's deputy vehicle was parked in the office lot and I'd walked him back to the car, figuring Tonya would be in the general area. As promised, I'd try to give her the opportunity to meet Don on a more casual basis.

Tonya sat on the front steps of the porch, looking through a box of lost-and-found valuables at the request of an elderly man. "Sorry sir, there's no wallet here... just some jewelry and sunglasses."

The old man's shoulders slumped as he held his wife's fragile hand and nodded.

"If you want to leave your name and number, I'll call you if someone turns it in." Tonya pulled out a pen and paper, writing down the information.

Don pulled out a couple of twenty-dollar bills and quietly handed it to the old man. "Enjoy the day with your lovely wife."

The elderly couple graciously accepted his offer and slowly shuffled hand in hand back to the fair.

"Don, you're going to go broke today giving all

your money away," I joked.

Tonya smiled at him with silent admiration.

Chevy and Gunner tore around the side of the building in a playful game of chase. I looked past them as they sped down a small hill on the dirt road behind the office and saw Jacob leaning on the side of the maintenance building, tossing a ball in the air as he called the dogs over. The four-legged friends raced over and engaged in a game of fetch with the businessman.

"Looks like Jacob's finally taking a break," Tonya said as she watched the dogs compete for his attention. "The man's been down there working non-stop for twenty-four hours straight over-seeing all the activities. By the looks of it, I'd say they've been making a ton of truck deals."

Big Diesel sure knew how to turn an engagement celebration into a money-making opportunity.

"I'll go get Chevy." I said, attempting to leave Don and Tonya alone for a couple minutes.

"Don't even bother. Jacob's not allowing anyone near the maintenance area except his own staff." Tonya shook her head. "Not even me."

"Okay," I said, half relieved. Tonya just blew her chance to be alone with Don and I was now off the hook.

"Do you two want to come in for a glass of lemonade?" She asked and turned toward the door. "I know I'm sure thirsty."

Well, maybe I wasn't off the hook just yet. The two of us followed Tonya into her office and she closed the door, locking it behind her.

"Let me just get these valuables back in the safe,

first."

Don and I glanced at each other as she walked behind her desk and opened a small door in the wall. An ancient looking safe with a huge dial was hidden behind the door, and Tonya bent over and rolled the combination lock between her fingers until the vault popped open.

As she placed the box of lost-and-found jewelry on the top shelf, a pile of fifty-dollar bills tumbled out onto the floor. The lower part of the safe was overflowing with cash.

"I've been shopping for a bigger safe, but they're so expensive these days..." Tonya mumbled as she stuffed the money back in the safe, causing another handful of bills to fall out.

"Geez, they're not selling trucks for cash out there, are they?" Don asked and eyed the money scattered on the floor.

"Heck no, this is just from the fair operations. Big Diesel owns all the food and game booths out there," Tonya said as she attempted to straighten the stacks of cash inside. "This was the safest place around here to store money for the weekend."

I sensed Don's body shift slightly and glanced over in time to catch him intently watching Tonya from behind as she closed the safe's door.

Maybe he does like her, I thought.

That is, until something shiny caught my eye and I realized what he was really looking at – a nine-millimeter handgun that sat on the top shelf in Tonya's safe.

"I'll see you ladies later," Don said, his body tensed. "I've got work to do."

Chapter 7

I got up extra early Monday morning to help Tonya cleanup around the campground before I started my own work-week later in the day, giving Chevy a chance to romp around with Gunner and burn off some extra energy. That wasn't the only reason though. I was eager to find out how the new dog park would progress after the weekend's profits.

By the time I arrived at eight a.m. the food and game vendors were already long gone, and all that remained of their presence were several garbage barrels overflowing with trash. Well, that and the smell of fried foods that still hung in the morning air.

The guys from Big Diesel's car dealership were busy removing the trucks off the back pasture and returning them to the car lot, a job that would probably take half the day.

I bounded into the campground lodge to congratulate Tonya and stopped in mid stride when I saw her leaning against the door-frame of her office holding her stomach. It looked as though she was barely able to stand up.

I gathered my wits about me and rushed over,

wrapped her arm around my shoulder and helped sit her down in the desk chair. "Tonya, what's wrong?"

Jacob burst through the office door before she had a chance to answer. He looked like he just stepped out of a men's clothing catalogue, as usual.

"Excuse us for a minute, Avery." Jacob said and pulled out a money bag. "I need to get the deposit over to the bank as soon as it opens. Big Diesel wants me to report our profits by noon..."

I was struck at how put together he looked even at this early hour. Not a hair out of place and not a wrinkle in his khakis or light blue polo shirt.

Tonya's heavy sobs interrupted my thoughts and tears poured down her cheeks.

"Tonya?" I couldn't figure out what was wrong.

She slowly spun the leather chair around, lifted her arm, and pointed at the open office safe. As Jacob and I stared inside, Tonya collapsed further into the soft chair, unable to speak.

The safe was empty, except for the gun.

"They even took the 'lost-and-found' jewelry," she whispered.

Jacob's eyes grew cold and held out his empty money bag. "Where's Big Diesel's money?"

"I don't know," Tonya said, her lips trembling. "I opened the safe this morning and it was empty."

"What do you mean, you don't know?" His face turned an ugly shade of red. "You guaranteed me you were the only one with the combination."

I instinctively took a step in front of Tonya's chair to put a barrier between the two.

"Don't try to play with me," Jacob hissed and pounded his fist on her desk. "You WILL have every penny of Big Diesel's money when I come back here at eleven o'clock – or you'll be going straight to jail."

He threw the money bag to the floor and stormed out of the office, slamming the door on the way out.

I ran to the window and watched Jacob stomp back down the hill to the maintenance building and his makeshift headquarters. My hand trembled as I pulled out my phone to call Don and gave Tonya a bit of advice.

"Don't touch anything."

Chapter 8

Tonya leaned on my shoulder as I walked her outside
for some fresh air and we climbed on the tailgate of
my truck, watching Sheriff's deputies file into her
office.   Sensing something was wrong, Gunner
jumped into the back of my truck and wouldn't leave
Tonya's side.

"How well do you know Jacob and Big Dooley?" I
asked, hoping they'd give her a break.

"Not well enough." She let out a breath and
watched the guys removing trucks from the back
pasture.   "I'd only seen Big Diesel on TV and met
Jacob when he came out to do the business deals."

"How much money are we talking about?"

"Way more than I've got," she said as tears filled
her eyes. "My dreams are gone."

Gunner whined and licked her cheek.

I stared at the ground and realized what she was
planning. Not only was her dog park in jeopardy, but
she might have to sell the campground to come up
with Big Diesel's money.

Tonya's father owned several rental properties on
North Carolina's coast and had plenty of money, but I

knew she'd never ask him for a dime. She'd paid her own way through school and bought this land real cheap, then spent the next ten years building it up little by little.

I racked my brain, trying to come up with ideas when two stern looking deputies approached. I hoped they had some good news, but their frowns revealed otherwise.

"Tonya Addison?"

"Yes?"

"You're wanted as an accomplice for the break in and robbery of Mr. Melvin Medlock's home."

"What?" Tonya exclaimed and grabbed Gunner's collar tight. "I've never even been inside his house!"

"Good try," the male deputy said and pulled out his handcuffs. "Your fingerprints were found inside the Medlock's safe."

"And your business address was found in the deceased suspect's pants pocket," the female deputy added.

My jaw slackened and I reached for the dog's collar as the deputies pulled Tonya from the tailgate. "I'll take care of Gunner."

Tonya's head dropped and her blond hair fell over her face. The handcuffs made a loud clicking noise as they were tightened around her wrists.

"Ms. Tonya Addison, you're under arrest..."

Chapter 9

Watching law enforcement officials remove items from my friend's office made my stomach turn and I decided to divert my attention and take the dogs on a walk. My mind always worked better when I was in motion and I wanted to come up with a plan to help Tonya.

Several short trails weaved their way around the campground property but I chose the one that led out behind the main lodge. The path started on the dirt road that led down the gentle slope past the maintenance building, then turned into a nice wide four wheeler path that made a big loop through the woods bordering Mel Medlock's property.

Something bothered me about Jacob Tanner's forcefulness and I wanted to get inside his make-shift office in the maintenance building. I whistled for the dogs and started down the road and they raced past, kicking up dust. They both took a detour and raced through the open door of the maintenance building and I seized the opportunity.

I jogged behind them and was within ten feet from making it through the door when a man's body suddenly appeared, filling the entire opening.

Jacob leaned against the doorframe and rubbed his chin. "What can I do for you, Avery?"

Thinking fast, I said, "I'm taking the dogs for a walk."

I leaned to the side and could see the dogs playing tug-o-war with a towel behind his legs. Jacob kept his eyes on mine as he stepped out from the doorway and whistled. Both dogs heeded his request and brought their tug game outside.

Jacob purposefully closed the door behind him, moved one step too close and towered over me. "What do you think happened to Big Diesel's money?"

I took a step backwards, away from his cologne, and watched him closely. "I was just going to ask you the same thing."

"Big Diesel will make sure ALL the guilty parties are prosecuted," he said and pointed to the dogs trotting down the trail. "Have a good walk."

*****

I was half mad and half scared after the encounter with Jacob and my heart raced. It ticked me off that he'd even insinuate that I knew anything about missing money, but Big Diesel had so much power that it made me nervous just the same. I worried what would happen if Jacob mentioned my name to his boss.

After all, it was impossible to believe Tonya had anything to do with a robbery and the deputies had already hauled her off to jail. I sure didn't want to be railroaded next. It took me a minute to realize that this train of thought wasn't going to help anything and I forced myself to snap out of it.

I watched the dogs run up and down the trail and gradually focused on studying the trail itself. My search and rescue thought process took over as a story written in the trail's dried mud revealed itself. There were three sets of tracks on this trail. A man's large boot track, a smaller sized boot track – probably from a woman and a set of dog's tracks.

I slowed and studied the tracks as the dogs were captivated by a smell in the bushes. Some of the prints were deep and sunk in, obviously made while the trail was soaked and muddy. The rest were shallow and recently made in the soft dirt while the trail was dry.

The only time the trail could have been muddy in recent weeks was the night of the robbery and shooting and only a few people even knew this trail existed. My stomach turned as I pulled out my smart phone, squatted down and took pictures of the deep imprints - the woman's boot prints and the dog tracks.

It just couldn't be. I'd known her for several years.

But... how well did I really know Tonya?

Chapter 10

You've got to be kidding me!

Things were in enough turmoil without coming home from work and finding over-flowing laundry baskets and a dryer that's conked-out. My back was in knots as I un-plugged and re-plugged the thing at least five times, read all the manual's trouble shooting tips and pushed every button available. Nothing worked.

It was dead. Like, rest in peace.

A power surge probably fried it during the storm the other day, I thought. Up here in the high country, lightning was no joke.

I knew it would cost at least a couple hundred dollars to even try and get it fixed. I also knew I didn't have two more weeks' worth of clean clothes to wear while I waited for a repairman to show up. Sighing heavily, I sucked it up and drove an hour to the city to buy a new one.

The only place that sold appliances this late in the day was Dower's Hardware Warehouse and I was getting desperate for something to go right. At least Dower's allowed dogs to come inside and shop and that was a positive, since I brought both Chevy and Gunner along for the ride.

I'd just gotten a system worked out for walking both dogs in a calm manner when Chevy yanked me straight over to the customer service desk. It'd been a month since our last visit, but my dog never forgot where the dog cookies were.

"Oh, Chevy's here!" a middle aged woman exclaimed and ran out from behind the counter to bury her face in my dog's golden fur and sneak him a handful of treats.

The other girls flew out from behind the service desk and Gunner jostled for his share of affection and snacks. It was like I was stuck in the pit stop at a car race and had to let Chevy fuel up before I was allowed to actually shop.

None of the ladies there actually knew my name, but they all sure knew my dog. I wasn't complaining – Chevy's popularity had gotten me a couple good deals in the past.

I finally made my way back to the appliance department and looked at a few drying machines, putting my hand in the tubs and spinning them around. It didn't take long to figure out I wasn't in the mood to shop and I quickly decided to buy the same model dryer I had at home. This would be the easiest sale the appliance guy had made all year.

An older guy with a wisp of white hair, a friendly demeanor and 'Jeff' on his nametag went to the stock room to check whether he had a new dryer, while I tried to entertain the two dogs. It was going well enough until an over-worked mother came in to shop with kids that had a lot more energy than she did.

She clung to the baby carrier in her shopping cart, cooing at an infant while the other kids ran in circles and clamored around her. It was apparent that she was out-numbered and in way over her head. The kids raced past us, giggling and darting in and out of the appliance displays. The dogs watched their every move and pranced in place, wanting to join in the fun.

Chevy started play barking and Gunner's eyes reflected the desire to herd the kids into the corner. The shortest kid ran by and wiped his chocolate covered hands across the front of one of the washing machines, leaving a brown streak in the process. My knuckles grew white as I gripped the dogs' leashes extra tight, just in case one of them decided to bolt.

Jeff, the sales guy stumbled back. "Sorry ma'am, I don't have one of those dryers in stock until Wednesday, but if you'd like to purchase the display I'll give you a ten percent discount."

I glanced at the chocolate stains on the display next to me and watched one of the older kid's kick another and decided I could wait another day or two to get a new one. There was plenty of rope at the house and I could put together a clothesline for a couple laundry sessions.

As I paid Jeff for my order, I asked, "Where can I get some clothespins?"

"Aisle fifteen," he said and pointed toward the other end of the massive store. "Would you like me to walk you over?"

"No, thanks. I'll find my way."

As I slowly walked down the broad cement aisle, I had a vision of Chevy playing tug-o-war with clothes drying on a line and hoped I'd made the right decision.

It's too late to change my mind now, I thought. I'd already passed up both the display dryer and the ten percent discount.

"Whoa, wait a minute." I said out loud to myself.

My heartbeat picked up and I jogged down the expansive aisles to the hardware department, with Chevy and Gunner keeping pace beside me. A young woman in a store vest was putting away a box of locks and I made a beeline directly to her. Startled, she took a step back as I approached at full speed.

"Do you sell safes?" I asked between heavy breaths.

"Yes, ma'am."

"Do you give a ten percent discount if it's a display?" I untangled the dog leashes.

She gave a slight frown. "Only if it's the last one we have in stock."

"Can you show me where they are, please?"

I followed the lady two aisles over and hurried past her when I saw the home safes. There was an empty spot in the display area.

"What about this one?" I looked at the tag and wrote down the description.

"We have more on the way." She patted the dogs on the head. "I sold the display a week or two ago."

"To who?"

She eyed me for a moment and hesitated. "An older military man, if I remember right."

I ran out of the store without saying good-bye.

The saleslady called behind me... "I can get you another model for the same price!"

*****

"Avery, I keep telling you to stay out of law enforcement investigations." Don sounded exasperated and it didn't bother me one bit.

"Just do me one favor." I stood in the hardware store's parking lot and opened the passenger door to my truck. "Check and see if Tonya's prints were ONLY found on the inside of Mr. Medlock's safe."

"You had dispatch radio me for that?"

"Listen, I think I know how her prints got in his safe." I loaded Chevy and Gunner inside so they could be in the air conditioning. "Mel Medlock just got a new safe and is very conservative with his money. I bet he recently bought the display model over at the hardware warehouse for a ten percent discount."

There was no response from Don. Crickets.

I shut the passenger door and circled the front of the truck to the driver's side. "Tonya's been looking for a new safe and recently shopped here, so she could've touched the inside of his safe at the store before he bought the display."

Don blew out a deep breath into the phone and said, "I'll check it out, but that's the least of her problems."

I frowned as Chevy licked my cheek. "What do you mean?"

"We've tested the gun found in her office safe." He paused. "It matches the bullet that killed Mr. Leonardo."

Chapter 11

"Boy, you sure are quiet today."

Don glanced at me as he fiddled with the keys, trying to figure out which one fit the door lock.

My eyes felt heavy even after two extra doses of caffeine. I hadn't gotten much sleep the night before, due to the battle raging in my mind about Tonya's situation. The girl I knew was neither a thief nor a murderer, despite the so-called evidence. Things just weren't adding up.

"Did she tell you where she stores the dog food?" Don asked as he opened the campground lodge door.

"It's in the mudroom."

Tonya used her free phone call at the jailhouse to give me instructions about caring for Gunner and asked that we get the dog's supplies. That was another first for me - getting a phone call from a prisoner. I guess I could mark that off my bucket list, if I had one.

As I stood in the doorway watching Don retrieve a twenty-pound bag of kibble from a storage bin, my eyes roamed to the old towels I'd hung on the hooks the evening of the murder and my heart sank. After all her hard work building up this campground, Tonya might very well lose this place.

I picked up one of the dry, stiff towels from the hook. "You know, Tonya was here for a meeting when you found the dead body."

"True." Don walked past me and lugged the dog food down the porch steps. "But according to the evidence, he was shot during the early afternoon. At least two hours before I found the body during the big thunderstorm."

"Hmmm. That would have been during the afternoon showers."

Don turned toward my truck.

I stood in the open doorway, glanced around the room one last time and was struck by a missing item.

"Wait just a minute."

Don groaned as he did a three-sixty and came back inside.

"When I hung these towels in here, Tonya and Jacob Tanner were meeting inside the office and a dripping raincoat was hanging right there." I pointed to the rung closest to the door.

"Makes sense, it was a rainy day," Don said and dropped the food bag at his feet.

"Yeah." I spun around and pointed toward the inside of the lodge. "But when Tonya ran out to meet you, she grabbed her rain jacket from the bed in the back room. It was dry."

Don pulled out his pad and took a couple notes. "So, Tonya wasn't outside during the time of the murder – or at least her coat wasn't."

"But Jacob was." I touched the empty rung on the wall. "That must've been his jacket."

I knew that didn't place him at the murder scene, but I hoped it might be enough to show the detectives - or a judge - that Tonya wasn't.

"I can look into it further," Don said and tried to usher me out the door.

"Something doesn't sit right with me about Jacob Tanner." I crossed my arms and held my position in the doorway. "He's too protective of that maintenance barn."

"I agree, but don't ask me to barge in there because I don't have cause." Don put his arm around my back and guided me out to the porch. "Let me lock this door so I can get back to the investigations, I've got two thefts and a murder to figure out."

I stood on the porch gathering my thoughts and watched as Don heaved the dog food bag into the back of my truck. Chevy and Gunner made me smile when they stuck their heads out the cab window, hoping he'd let them out to play. Then it hit me.

I know who can spy on Jacob for me

Chapter 12

"Come here, Chevy."

The dogs scrambled out of the truck and I leaned in the front passenger seat, pulling out the gift Tonya had given me a few days before. I peeked over the roof of my truck to make sure Don had driven all the way out of the campground, quickly re-read the doggie cam instructions, hooked the camera on Chevy's collar and made sure it was ready to record.

"Okay buddy, we may have only one shot at this," I said and gave my dog a quick hug.

Avery, this is ridiculous. My own doubt tried to snuff out my idea before I even had a chance to carry out my plan.

I forced the negative thoughts aside and joined the dogs at the back of the truck, making big circles with my throwing arm to loosen up. Both dogs pranced at my feet, intently watching the tennis ball in my hand and vying for the best position.

"Haven't played softball since high school, but I've still got the touch." I chuckled to the dogs and did a couple jumping jacks for good measure.

My plan was to entice Jacob to let the dogs in the

maintenance barn so Chevy's dog-cam could record a video of the secret office. I tossed the ball in the air a couple of times, wound up like a pro baseball pitcher and lunged.

The tennis ball flew through the air, hit the dirt path and bounced down the hill towards the maintenance building. Chevy raced after the ball, his golden fur floating in the air, with Gunner hot on his trail.

Both dogs skidded to a stop at the bottom of the hill, kicking up a cloud of dust and Chevy grabbed the ball just as Gunner stretched out to snatch it. The Border Collie decided he wouldn't come up second twice and raced back to me ready for the next throw. Chevy arrived shortly after, squeezing his teeth into the tennis ball with pride.

That didn't work too well, I thought.

Jacob's face appeared in the doorway of his temporary office and it gave me a glimmer of hope.

I threw the ball harder this time and the dogs tore down the dirt drive past the building. Gunner made the grab and Jacob whistled for the dogs to come over. He tossed the ball for the dogs a couple times then went into his make-shift office, the dogs trotting in behind him.

Jackpot. I smiled and hoped Jacob didn't notice the camera hanging from Chevy's collar. *Even if he does, he can't say anything... Chevy's just trying out his new toy.*

I moved to the chairs on the porch so as not to act suspicious. About a half-hour later the two dogs sauntered around the corner of the lodge, came up on the porch and drank from the water bowl. I unclipped the camera from Chevy's collar and held it up in triumph.

"Good job doggies, let's see what this guy is really up to."

The dogs followed me back into the cabin lodge and straight to Tonya's office. I locked the door, fired up her computer and stuck in the dog-cam USB. At first the video from Chevy's collar-cam bounced all over as he chased after the ball.

I blinked my eyes to keep from getting dizzy watching the thing.

Eventually, it got to the interesting part. Jacob walked into the maintenance building and the video capture followed him at knee level. A big hand comes into view holding some dog treats, which disappear with one bite.

"That's just like you, Chevy," I laughed. "No wonder you two dogs keep going in there."

The dog-cam surprisingly took really clear video.

I made a mental note to thank Tonya again for the great present and returned my focus to the video.

My eyes squinted as I noticed something unusual, reached up and touched the computer screen. Sitting on a folding table behind Jacob were a box of latex medical gloves.

What would he need those for?

As the video continued, Chevy got a scratch on the head then trotted over to a complete stranger and plopped down on the cool concrete floor, watching as the bearded man swept a pile of wallets and credit cards off a table and into a backpack.

Pick pocketing!

I *knew* something fishy had been going on down

there.

My finger pressed pause on the computer just before my thumb speed dialed Don.

Don answered on the first ring and didn't bother to say hello. "Avery, will you let me get back to work on this investigation?"

I looked at the phone and frowned. "Yeah, I'd be happy to. Get back over here and look at this new evidence I've got for you."

*****

Don leaned in close to the computer screen. "There were several reports of wallets missing during the festival." He looked closer. "That's Donny D. We arrested him a couple times last year for pickpocketing."

"I had fifty bucks disappear," I said, now even more miffed at Jacob.

Don glanced at me. "How did you get this video?"

"Chevy wanted to try out the gift Tonya gave us." I opened my hands and gave him my best innocent look. "The dogs just happened to go in the maintenance barn while the camera was rolling."

"Hmmm." Don returned his focus to the computer screen.

Gunner photo-bombed the video as he did a play bow, trying to get Chevy to play. There were more dizzying chase scenes until Chevy trotted over to Jacob and tried to stick his nose into an over-sized duffle bag just as the man dumped an armful of cash inside.

Don stopped the video. "I thought they stored all the cash up here."

"They did." My face grew hot as I recalled how

Jacob bullied Tonya about the missing money.

"A set up – Jacob steals the money and blames Tonya." Don leaned back and glared at the computer screen. "Then he tries to force Tonya into repaying the money to Big Diesel. If she can't pay it off, she ends up in jail and they claim it on insurance."

"He keeps the money and Big Diesel is taken care of either way." I nodded and pressed the heels of my hands into my eyes.

Don studied the frozen video screen with money pouring out of Jacob's arms.

"A double set up." He snapped his fingers and pointed at the screen. "There's more cash there than what could fit in Tonya's safe."

I opened the secret door behind the desk to double check the size of her safe.

Don stood and reached for his radio. "Maybe his guys robbed both Mel Medlock and Tonya's safe."

"...and pick pocketed half the crowd at the fair," I added.

Don nodded in agreement. "Let me get some help out here. Lock up, will you?"

"But..." I followed him outside.

"There's still the issue of Tonya's gun and the murder." Don spoke to me, but his eyes stayed on the maintenance barn. "The gun was stored in her safe and she's already admitted that no one else had the combination."

My shoulders slumped as I let out a disappointed breath. Don was right about the safe. It was still sitting in Tonya's office, unharmed.

No matter how hard I tried, the evidence kept leading back to Tonya.

Chapter 13

I collapsed into Tonya's office chair as I listened to Jacob Tanner's truck race past the lodge and down the driveway, followed by his buddies. I heard a siren in the distance and figured either Don or one of the deputies pulled the whole crowd over.

Soon after, another deputy car flew down the dirt road and skidded to a stop at the maintenance building. I sat in the office chair and stared at the screen for a minute, then hit 'play' to view the rest of Chevy's video. There wasn't much more to it, Jacob shooed Chevy away from the money bags and the dogs headed back outside.

My phone rang and I picked up, keeping my eye on the doggie cam video footage of Gunner and Chevy playing on the foot path outside the maintenance shed. Mostly I saw close-ups of Gunner's animated face as the two wrestled.

"Jacob didn't have the money in his truck and is playing dumb," Don said. "The guys are still hunting for the other two that flew out of the campground."

He was interrupted by dispatch and after a moment, continued, "The maintenance barn has been cleared out. The way they all took off out of there, it seems like they were tipped off."

"What are you saying? There's no one here to tip them off, Don." I looked past the computer and teddy bear sitting on Tonya's desk at the napping dogs. "It was just us."

"Calm down, I wasn't accusing you of anything."

"Right, so that leaves the dogs and a teddy bear."

"Huh?"

"The teddy bear Jacob left for Tonya..." The hair on the back of my neck stood up as I stared at the little bear. I picked up the cute toy and squeezed its soft belly. Something reflected back at me and I took a closer look.

"You've gotta be kidding me..." I yelled. I was so upset, so enraged that I jolted back too far and flipped backwards out of the chair.

*****

Don bolted through the office door and found me lying on the floor rubbing my head, hugging a teddy bear and surrounded by two worried dogs.

I looked up as he bent over the top of me. "He did it the same way I did."

"What?"

"It's one of those bears with a tiny hidden camera inside." I reached up and handed him the teddy bear. "It's been sitting on Tonya's desk pointed right at the safe combination lock."

Don studied the stuffed bear. "This is one high tech piece of equipment."

"Jacob just waited and watched until Tonya opened the safe and was able to get the combination. He had plenty of time to stash the gun back in her safe while she helped me get some dry clothes the other night. He also had full access all weekend during the festival."

"And he probably just saw us watching the dog cam video." Don reached out and helped me to my feet. "That just leaves one question... where's the money?"

Chapter 14

My hiking boots kicked up dust as I walked down the hill to the maintenance building. I wanted to take a look around the place for myself. Chevy and Gunner played tug-o-war in the doorway and two deputies were elbowing each other in the ribs. I'd never seen grown men giggling like that before, at least not while they were in uniform.

"Ooh, Tonya's gonna be mad at you Chevy. Those fancy ones are expensive."

I walked up to the dogs to see what had the deputies so intrigued. Gunner and Chevy were playing tug with a brand new lacy white bra. The tags from an expensive lingerie shop were still attached and an empty gift box lay on the ground next to them.

"Hey, let go."

Gunner obeyed, letting loose of his end of the undergarment while Chevy kept hold of his, causing the elastic band to snap back and shoot the end of the bra onto Chevy's head.

The deputies' laughs grew even louder.

"That looks like you on a Saturday night," the young deputy ribbed the older one.

"Give me that, Chevy." He dropped the bra in my hand. "Where'd you get that, anyway?"

Once I had the material in my hand, it was immediately apparent that it didn't belong to Tonya. She had an athletic figure and who ever owned this item was, could you say, extra gifted.

"What were those guys doing in here all weekend, entertaining a bunch of ladies and buying them gifts?" The young deputy tried to stifle his laughter and stepped inside the building looking for more clues.

I looked down the path at the deep tracks made in the mud during the recent storm. "Not a bunch of ladies, just one well-endowed one." I raced down the path and called out behind me, "Follow me!"

All the foot prints back and forth on this path suddenly made sense. They weren't from Tonya's shoes, they were created by the woman. The intended recipient of Jacob's gift.

I followed the deep tracks where they cut through a gap in the woods and popped out near the back door of the Medlock's double-wide mobile home. Mel, ever on the alert since the robbery, burst out his back door with a hunting rifle trained on me.

Heather Medlock clung to her husband's waist from behind and announced, "I told you that girl had been following me. She's friends with that thief, Tonya."

"You've arrived on private property, ma'am," Mel said and got in a shooting stance. "And if you move a muscle, you won't be leaving here alive."

I knew Mel's skills and one shot would be all it'd take to send me to heaven.

"Call the cops, Heather," he looked over his shoulder.

Heather started pacing. "She robbed us Mel, shoot her."

"No, I didn't..."

I was interrupted when the older deputy almost knocked me over as he staggered out of the woods, wheezing and holding his chest. Mel lowered his gun and held it behind the doorframe when he saw the deputy, but he didn't put it down.

I tried not to move a muscle and spoke to the deputy. "Jacob Tanner had a lock down on the maintenance building for more reasons than the money his team was stealing."

The deputy looked from person to person.

"Mel's wife is the only one I know that could fit that bra," I continued.

"Oh. Ohhhh." The deputy finally figured it out and radioed his team.

Chevy and Gunner flew out of the woods into the backyard, went up to Heather and begged for a handout. A dead giveaway - she'd probably been giving them treats when they visited Jacob's office.

Heather realized her secret was out and grabbed her husband's gun. As if in slow motion, she took a pot shot in my direction. I dove to the ground and rolled. The loud noise right next to their ears startled the dogs and Gunner jumped up, pawing at Heather's arm. Worried about the dogs, I got back to my feet and ran toward her as the deputy pulled his weapon.

Mel grabbed the gun and threw it to the ground. "Are you trying to get us killed?"

As Don and the other deputy's surrounded

Heather to place her in custody, I tried to tell the rest of the story.

"Heather's been using this trail to visit Jacob at the maintenance building. And I'll bet she shot D. Leonardo using Tonya's gun."

Mel stared from me to his wife and back again. "Why would my little lady do something like that?" Mel questioned, glaring at me.

"Because...." I looked him straight in the eye. "Leonardo messed up when he didn't kill you."

Chapter 15

Deputies searched the Medlock's house and walked out with a duffle bag full of cash. Mel Medlock swore up and down that he didn't know anything about it and I believed him. Once Jacob was arrested and learned his hot girlfriend was trying to pin a murder on him, he rolled over like a trick pony.

Jacob and Heather had been having an affair and decided to take it to another level. Heather decided she wanted a new man without being bogged down by another ex. The hot looking woman came up with a cold blooded plan that, surprisingly, almost worked.

After all the investigations, Don explained it to me something like this:

Heather hired a known pickpocket and some of his buddies to work the crowd at the fair and offered an extra bonus. One of them was talked into robbing Mel's safe and was supposed to kill Mel with Tonya's gun in the process. That way, Heather would get the death benefits, the cash from the safe and her new man, Jacob.

When the pickpocket couldn't upgrade to murder, Heather wouldn't let that derail her dream and she shot the thief at close range in her front yard. The man later staggered up the road, finally collapsing at Tonya's gate.

With Tonya blamed for theft and murder, she'd have to sell off her land quickly and Heather would be ready to buy it at a cheap price.... the same amount that Tonya owed Big Diesel... because Jacob and Heather had stolen that money too.

It almost worked, until two dogs played tug-o-war with a bra.

*****

Over the next couple weeks, every single person who reported missing money at the festival received a new wallet in their mailbox stuffed with five hundred dollars and a handwritten apology from Big Diesel... along with a seven hundred dollar coupon for a discount off a new truck from his dealership.

Don delivered my new wallet from Big Diesel in person. I sat on my front porch in the rocking chair, inspected the contents and chuckled. "That guy knows how to turn anything into a selling opportunity."

It was just like Big Diesel to step in and make things right, even if none of it was his fault.

As for Tonya? The generous car dealer insisted she get double her cut of the festival profits and promised to pick up the tab on the campground's new dog park. And of course, he'd spare no expense.

Two months later, Tonya cut the ribbon on the park with a grand celebration. It was rightly named The Triple D.

About The Author

Mary Hiker spent her childhood rescuing animals, playing in the outdoors and reading Nancy Drew Mysteries. Fast forward quite a few years and her books reflect the passions that started in her youth.

She now lives in the western North Carolina mountains and spends lots of time in the forest enjoying nature. Mary is a true animal lover and her own dogs are the inspiration behind Chevy's hijinks in the Avery Barks Dog Mysteries series.

You can visit Mary at her website and sign up for her Newsletter to be notified when new books are released.

www.maryhiker.com